This dragon book belongs to:

....

Fix Your Dragon's Attitude
My Dragon Books - Volume 18
Written by Steve Herman

ISBN: 978-1948040501 (paperback)
ISBN: 978-1948040525 (hardcover)

www.MyDragonBooks.com

First Edition: September 2018

10 9 8 7 6 5 4 3 2 1

Fix Your Dragon's Attitude

My Dragon Books - Volume 18

Steve Herman

That's right! He is a dragon –
His name is Diggory Doo,
And though he's very good,
this wasn't always true.

I regret I must admit it,
but it simply is a fact –
When Diggory Doo was little,
he did not know how to act!

When Diggory had to do a thing he did not want to do, He'd pout and stomp his foot, and loudly cry, "Boo Hoo!"

When it was time to brush his teeth at bedtime every night, Diggory made excuses and would put up quite a fight.

"Why must I brush my baby teeth,
when they will just fall out,
Then new ones grow to take their place?"
Diggory Doo would shout.

Of all the classes Diggory took
every day at school,
He hated history class the most;
he said it wasn't cool.

When Diggory Doo had homework,
you should hear how he'd protest!
"I work all day at school,
so at home, I want to rest"

Then Diggory Doo complained again -
He got it in his head...
That his friend no longer liked him
or preferred new friends instead.

Diggory Doo complained again,
"Whatever shall I do?
I guess I'll get my video game out
and play a game or two."

Then Diggory Doo complained once more,
for much to his dismay
His TV set was broken,
so he could not play!

"Diggory Doo," I told him, "I really think you should Not dwell upon the *bad* in life, but *focus* on the good."

"All you ever do is grumble;
it's depressing and it's rude.
If you want to have a better life,
then change your ATTITUDE."

Sometimes bad things happen,
but in every situation,
If you change your point of view,
you'll find cause for celebration.

I said, "Diggory, do your homework, and don't throw such a fit. Teacher doesn't give you much - just a tiny little bit."

"When a friend cannot come out to play, why must you assume... That he no longer likes you and hang your head in gloom?"

"Perhaps his mother gave him chores -
who knows what it could be...
Or maybe he's not feeling well -
Just ask him and you'll see."

"There are better things that you can do to drive the blues away - For instance, it's much healthier to go outside and play."

He thought it over for a bit,
then Diggory Doo agreed -
"An attitude adjustment
is exactly what I need!"

POSITIVITY

"If I change my state of mind, I change my life, as well." – That's exactly what he did; now Diggory's feeling swell!

The world is such a lovely place
everywhere you look -
Diggory sees it clearly now -
a minor change is all it took.

Do you need an attitude adjustment?
Just change your point of view;
If Diggory Doo can do it,
then you can do it, too!

Read more about Drew and Diggory Doo!

Visit
www.MyDragonBooks.com
for more!